SCOOP!

an EXCLUSIVE by
MONTY MOLENSKI

additional words and pictures by
John Kelly and Cathy Tincknell

THE DAILY ROAR

SCOOP!

ILL-FATED FÊTE!
CAKE COMPETITION ENDS IN CONTAMINATION

Ace reporter Chris Croc brings you a slice of the action!

CAKE FÊTE

DANGER: KEEP OUT

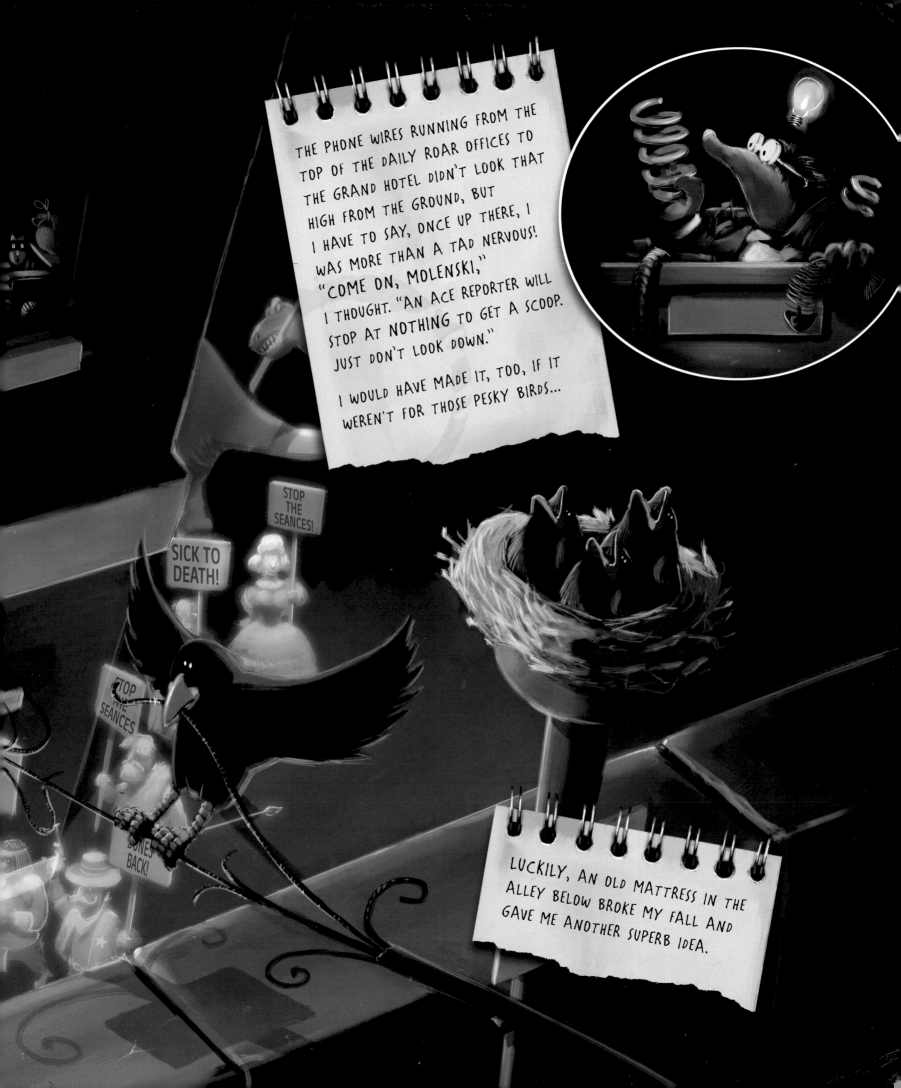

THE PHONE WIRES RUNNING FROM THE
TOP OF THE DAILY ROAR OFFICES TO
THE GRAND HOTEL DIDN'T LOOK THAT
HIGH FROM THE GROUND, BUT
I HAVE TO SAY, ONCE UP THERE, I
WAS MORE THAN A TAD NERVOUS!
"COME ON, MOLENSKI,"
I THOUGHT. "AN ACE REPORTER WILL
STOP AT NOTHING TO GET A SCOOP.
JUST DON'T LOOK DOWN."

I WOULD HAVE MADE IT, TOO, IF IT
WEREN'T FOR THOSE PESKY BIRDS...

STOP
THE
SEANCES!

SICK TO
DEATH!

STOP
THE
SEANCES

BONES
BACK!

LUCKILY, AN OLD MATTRESS IN THE
ALLEY BELOW BROKE MY FALL AND
GAVE ME ANOTHER SUPERB IDEA.

BACK ON THE ROOF OF THE DAILY ROAR, I TOOK A DEEP BREATH AND LAUNCHED MYSELF INTO SPACE WEARING MY NEW 'GRAVITY-DEFYING MOLENSKI SPRING-BOOTS'. UNFORTUNATELY, THE SPRINGS WERE A TEEEEEENSY BIT MORE POWERFUL THAN I'D CALCULATED. INSTEAD OF LANDING ON THE ROOF OF THE GRAND HOTEL, I OVERSHOT IT RATHER, AND ALMOST ENDED UP IN THE BOATING LAKE.

IT'S GOING TO BE A **LONG** WALK BACK.

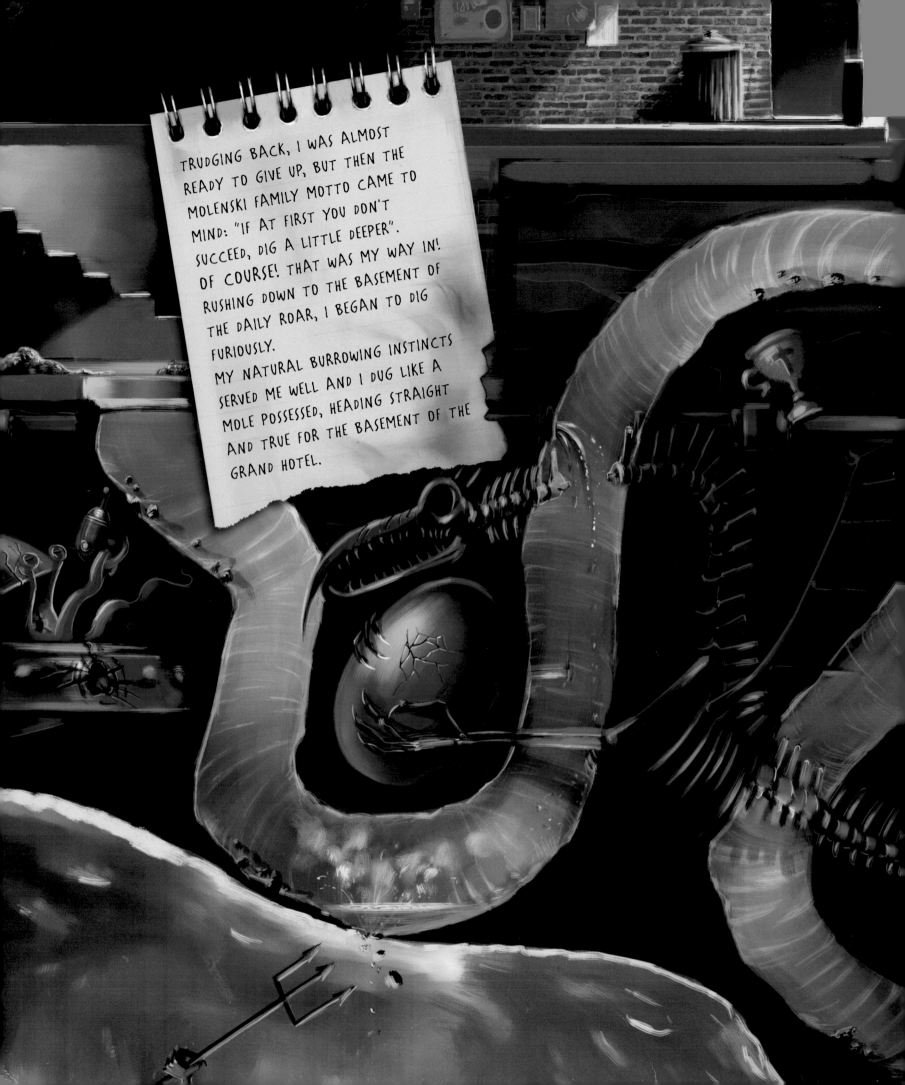

TRUDGING BACK, I WAS ALMOST
READY TO GIVE UP, BUT THEN THE
MOLENSKI FAMILY MOTTO CAME TO
MIND: "IF AT FIRST YOU DON'T
SUCCEED, DIG A LITTLE DEEPER".
OF COURSE! THAT WAS MY WAY IN!
RUSHING DOWN TO THE BASEMENT OF
THE DAILY ROAR, I BEGAN TO DIG
FURIOUSLY.
MY NATURAL BURROWING INSTINCTS
SERVED ME WELL AND I DUG LIKE A
MOLE POSSESSED, HEADING STRAIGHT
AND TRUE FOR THE BASEMENT OF THE
GRAND HOTEL.

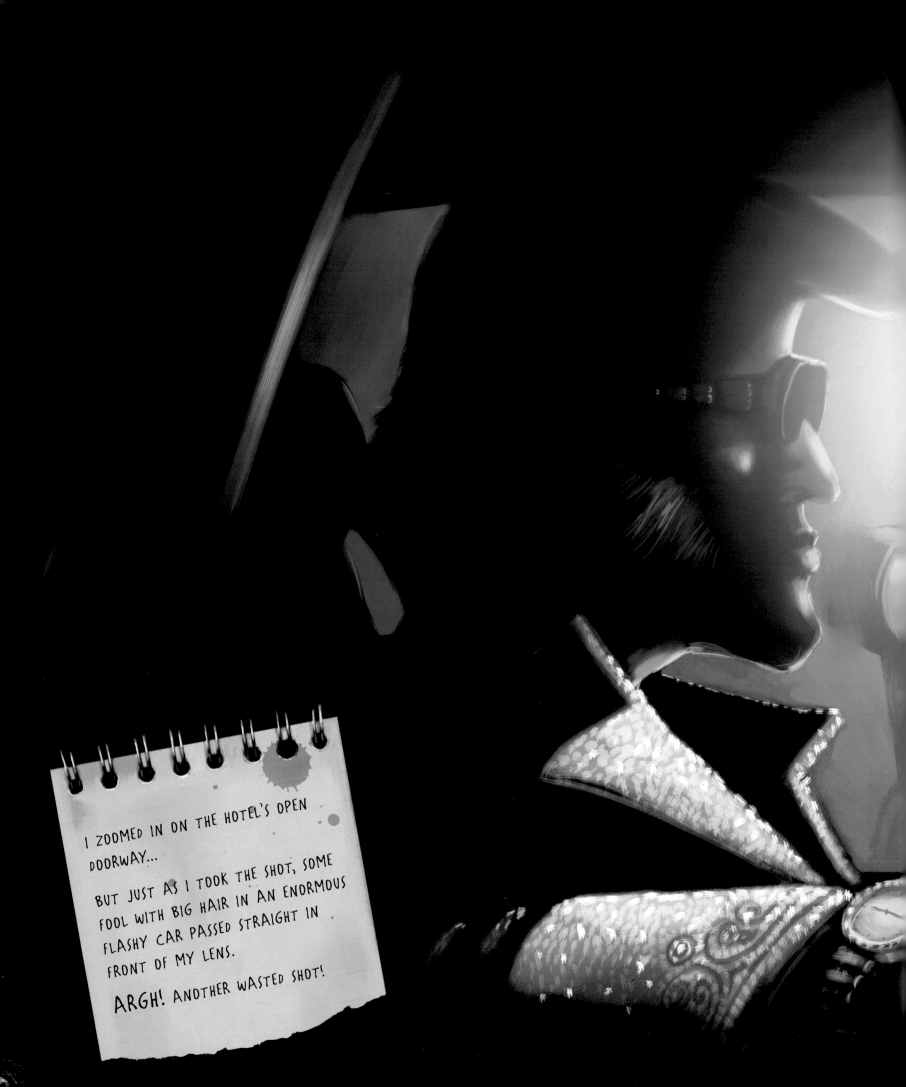

click!

BY THE TIME THE CAR HAD PASSED BY, THE ONLY PICTURE I COULD GET WAS OF CHRIS CROC AND THE OTHER REPORTERS LEAVING. NOT REALLY FRONT PAGE MATERIAL. WHAT HAD THEY BEEN UP TO IN THERE?

THEN I SAW IT: MY CHANCE TO GET IN. THE DOORMAN WAS DISTRACTED, THE DOOR LEFT OPEN, AND WITH THE NIMBLE SPEED OF A MOUNTAIN GOAT, I SNEAKED IN BEHIND HIS BACK.

THE MYSTERY IS ABOUT TO BE SOLVED!

DARKROOM
THE DAILY ROAR
ALL CAMERAS MUST BE LEFT HERE FOR OVERNIGHT PROCESSING
-THE NITE OWL
THOROUGHLY FED UP. RETURNED TO THE DESERTED DAILY ROAR OFFICES TO DROP OFF MY CAMERA AT THE NITE OWL'S FILM DEVELOPMENT LAB AS USUAL.
WHAT A WASTE OF TIME. OH, WELL. HOME TO BED.

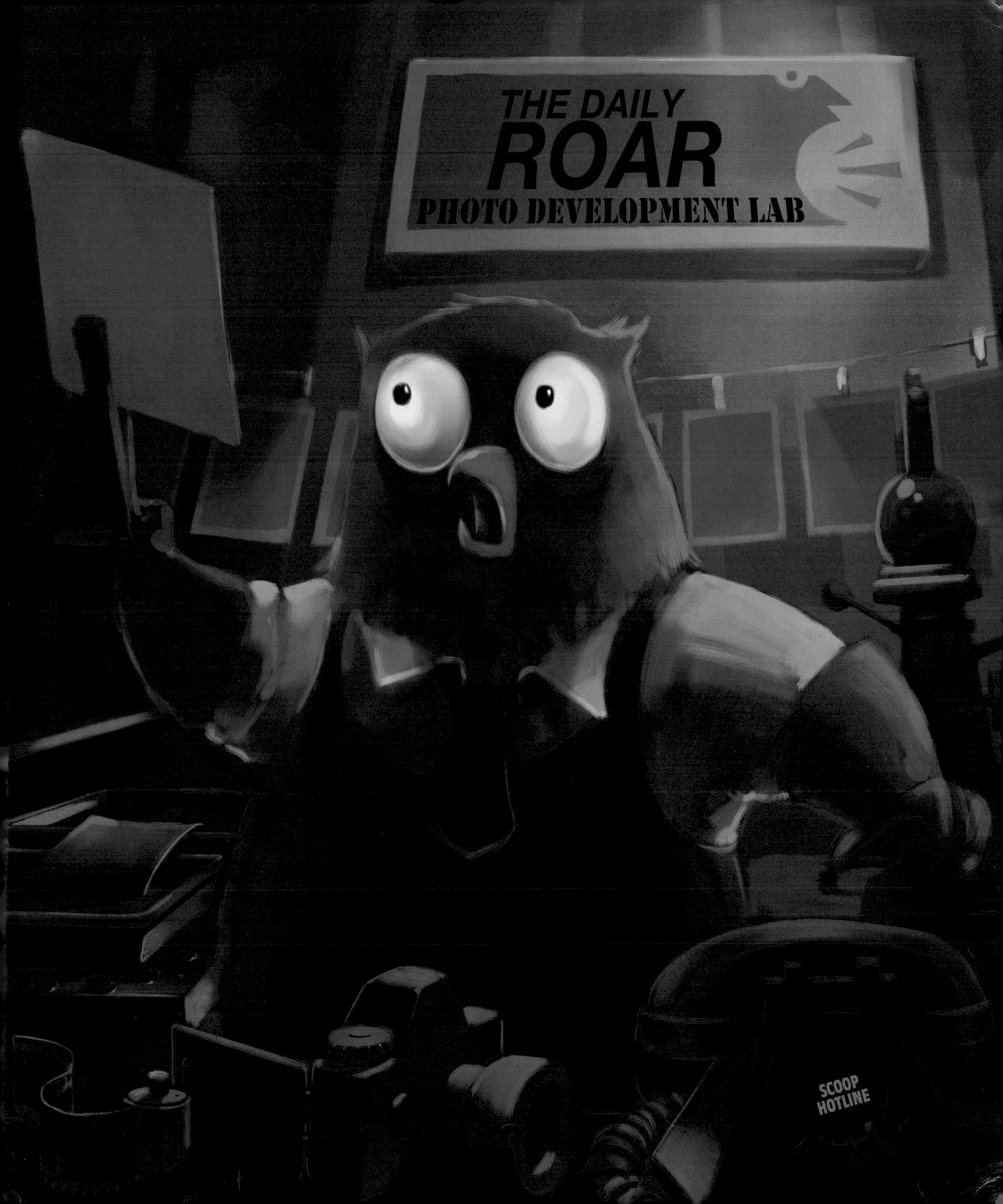
THE DAILY
ROAR
PHOTO DEVELOPMENT LAB
SCOOP
HOTLINE

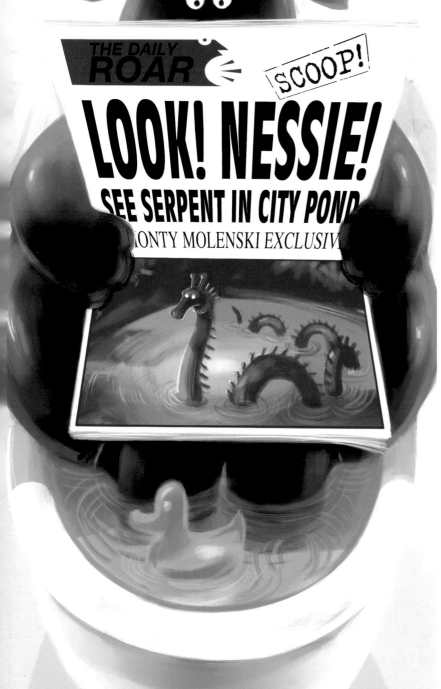

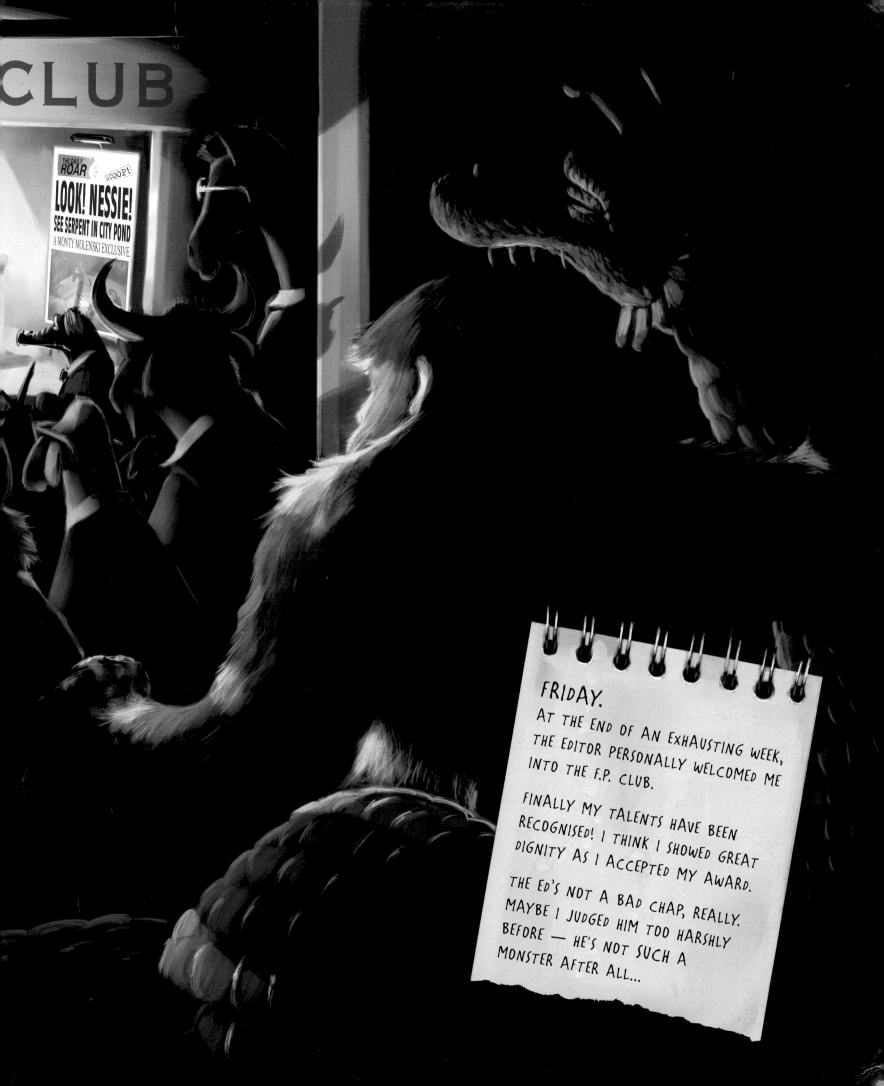

THE END?